*For Niamh*

Library of Congress Cataloging-in-Publication Data
Peachey, Caroline.
The Snow Queen/Hans Christian Andersen;
illustrated by P. J. Lynch; retold from the original
English version by Caroline Peachey. — 1st U.S. ed.
p.   cm.
Adaption of: Snedronningen.
"First published, 1993, by Andersen Press" — T.p. verso.
"Gulliver books."
Summary: After the Snow Queen abducts her friend Kay,
Gerda sets out on a perilous and magical journey to find him.
ISBN 0-15-200874-8
[1. Fairy tales.]   I. Lynch, Patrick James, ill.
II. Andersen, H. C. (Hans Christian), 1805–1875.
Snedronningen.   English.   III. Title.
PZ8.P2856Sn   1994
[Fic]—dc20     93-42711

A B C D E

Printed and bound in Italy

HANS CHRISTIAN ANDERSEN

# THE
# SNOW QUEEN

## Illustrated by P. J. LYNCH

*Retold from the original English version by Caroline Peachey*

GULLIVER BOOKS
HARCOURT BRACE & COMPANY
San Diego    New York    London

# THE MIRROR
# AND ITS FRAGMENTS

There was once a wicked troll who was more wicked than anybody else. One day he was in a very happy frame of mind for he had just constructed a mirror that made everything good and beautiful shrink up to nothing when it was reflected in it, but all those things that were ugly and useless were magnified and made to appear ten times worse than before. In this mirror, the loveliest landscapes looked like boiled spinach and the most beautiful people appeared odious. Their features were so distorted that their friends could never recognize them. Moreover, if one of them had a freckle it seemed to spread right over his nose and mouth; and if a good thought glanced across his mind, a wrinkle was seen in the mirror. The troll thought all this was highly entertaining, and he chuckled at his clever work.

The goblins who studied at the school of magic where he taught spread the fame of this wonderful mirror, and said that for the first time the world and its inhabitants could be seen as they really were. They carried the mirror from place to place, until at last there was no country or person that had not been misrepresented in it. Then they flew up to the sky with it, to see if they could carry on their fun there. But the higher they flew, the more wrinkled the mirror became; they could scarcely hold it together. They flew on and on, higher and higher, until at last the mirror trembled so much that it escaped from their hands and fell to the earth, breaking into a million, billion little pieces. And then it caused far greater unhappiness than before, for fragments of it scarcely as large as grains of sand flew about in the air and got into people's eyes, making them see everything the wrong way and have eyes only for what was perverted and corrupt. For each little fragment retained the peculiar properties of the whole mirror. Some people were unfortunate enough to get little splinters into their hearts and that was disastrous for their hearts became cold and hard, like lumps of ice. The wicked troll was greatly amused with all this and he laughed till his sides ached.

Very soon we shall hear more about some of the little splinters of this mischievous mirror which were flying about in the air.

# A LITTLE BOY
# AND A LITTLE GIRL

 In a large town where there were so many houses that there was not room for every family to have a garden of its own and many people had to be content with keeping a few plants in pots, there lived two poor children named Gerda and Kay who shared a garden that was somewhat larger than a flowerpot. They were not brother and sister, but they loved each other just as much as if they had been. Their families lived in two attics that were exactly opposite each other. The roof of one house nearly joined the other, the gutter ran along between them, and there was a little window in each roof, so that you could stride across the gutter from one window to the other. Each family had a large wooden box in which they grew herbs for the kitchen, and they put these boxes on the gutter, so that they almost touched each other. A beautiful little rose tree grew in each box; scarlet runners entwined their long shoots over the windows and formed a flowery arch across the street. The children often used to sit on little stools under the rose trees, and thus they passed many a happy hour.

When winter came this wasn't possible anymore. The windows were often frozen over, and then the children heated half-pennies on the stove, held the warm coins against the frozen panes, and made little peepholes through which they could see each other.

In summer Gerda and Kay could climb out of their windows and jump over to each other quite easily. But in winter there were stairs to run down and stairs to run up while outside the wind roared and the snow fell.

"Those are the white bees swarming there," said Gerda's grandmother one winter day.

"Have they a queen bee?" asked Kay, for he knew that real bees have one.

"They have," said the grandmother. "She flies about over there where they swarm so thickly. She is the largest of them all and she never stays on the earth but flies up again into the black cloud. Sometimes on a winter's night she goes through the streets of the town and breathes with her frosty breath on the windows, covering them with strange and beautiful forms like trees and flowers."

"Yes, I have seen them!" said both the children, so they knew that this was true.

"Can the Snow Queen come in here?" asked Gerda.

"If she comes in," said Kay, "I'll put her on the hot stove, and then she'll melt."

And Gerda's grandmother stroked Kay's hair and told the children other stories.

That same evening, after Kay had gone home and was half undressed, he crept onto the chair by the window and peeped through the little round hole. Just then a few snowflakes fell outside and one, the largest of them, remained lying on the edge of one of the flowerpots. The snowflake grew larger and larger and at last took the form of a lady dressed in the finest silk, her robes made up of millions of starlike particles.

She was exquisitely fair and delicate but entirely made of ice—glittering, dazzling ice. Her eyes gleamed like two bright stars, but there was no rest in them. She nodded at the window and beckoned with her hand. Kay was frightened and jumped down from the chair to hide, but afterward he thought he saw something like a large bird fly past the window.

There was a clear frost next day, and soon afterward spring came. The trees and flowers budded, the swallows built their nests, the windows were opened, and the children sat once more in their little garden upon the gutter that ran along the roofs of the houses.

That summer the roses blossomed so beautifully that Gerda learned a hymn in which there was something about roses. It reminded her of her own. So she sang it to Kay, and he sang it with her.

*Our roses bloom and fade away,*
*Our Infant Lord abides always;*
*May we be blessed His face to see,*
*And ever little children be!*

And the children held each other by the hand, kissed the roses, and looked up into the blue sky, talking away all the time.

What glorious summer days those were. How wonderful it was to sit under those rose trees, which looked as though they never intended to stop flowering!

One day Kay and Gerda were sitting looking at their picture books full of birds and animals, when suddenly Kay exclaimed, "Oh, dear! What was that shooting pain in my heart, and oh, something has gone into my eye!"

Gerda turned and looked at him. He blinked his eyes; no, there was nothing to be seen.

"I think it has gone," said he, but it had not. It was one of those glass splinters from the magic mirror, the wicked glass that made everything great and good appear little and hateful, and that magnified everything ugly and mean. Poor Kay had a splinter too in his heart and it became hard and cold like a lump of ice. He no longer felt the pain, but the splinter was there.

"Why are you crying?" he asked. "You look ugly when you cry! There is nothing the matter with me. Oh!" he exclaimed again. "This rose has an insect in it. And just look at this! They are ugly roses after all, and it is an ugly box they grow in!" Then he kicked the box and tore off the roses.

"Oh, Kay, what are you doing?" cried Gerda. But when he saw how it upset her, he tore off another rose and jumped down through his own window, away from his once dear friend.

Ever afterward, when she brought out a picture book he called it a baby's book, and when her grandmother told stories, he interrupted with a "but," and sometimes he would get behind her grandmother, put on her spectacles, and speak just as she did. He did this in a very funny manner, and so people laughed at him. Very soon Kay could mimic everybody in the street and particularly everything that was distinctive and awkward about them, until his neighbors said, "What a remarkable brain that boy has!" But no, it was the glass splinter that had fallen into his eye and the glass splinter that had pierced his heart. It was these that made him not care whose feelings he hurt and even made him tease little Gerda.

He played quite different games now from the ones he had played before. One winter's day when it snowed he came out with a big magnifying glass and held it against his coat where the snowflakes fell on it.

"Now look at the glass, Gerda," he said.

Every flake of snow was magnified and looked like a beautiful flower or ten-pointed star. "See how clever they are!" Kay said. "They're much more interesting than real flowers and their design is absolutely flawless."

Soon after he came in with thick gloves on his hands and his sled slung across his back. He called out to Gerda, "I've got permission to play on the great square where the other boys are," and off he went.

The boldest boys in the square thought it particularly good fun to fasten their sleds onto the wagons of the country people and get pulled behind them. While they were in the middle of the game, a large sleigh painted white passed by; in it sat a person wrapped in a rough white fur, wearing a rough white cap. When the sleigh had driven twice round the square, Kay bound his little sled to it and was carried on with it. On they went, faster and faster, into the next street. The person driving the sleigh turned round and nodded kindly to Kay, just as if they were old friends, and every time Kay was going to loose his little sled, the person turned and nodded again, as if to signify that he must stay. So Kay sat still and they passed through the gates of the town. Then the snow began to fall so thickly that Kay could not see his own hand, but still he was carried on. He tried hastily to undo the cords and free himself from the sleigh, but it was no use; it wouldn't come undone, and he was carried on, swift as the wind. Then he cried out as loudly as he could, but no one heard him. The snow fell and the sleigh dashed on. Every now and then it sprang up as if it were bouncing over the top of the hedges and ditches. He was very frightened. He would have said a prayer, but the only things he could remember were his multiplication tables.

The snowflakes seemed to be getting larger and larger, till at last they looked like great white birds. All at once they parted, the large sleigh stopped, and the person who drove it rose from the seat. Kay saw that the cap and coat were made of snow and that the driver was a lady, tall and slender, and dazzlingly white. It was the Snow Queen!

"We have driven fast," she said, "but no one likes to be frozen. Creep under my bearskin." And she seated him in the sleigh by her side and spread her cloak around him. Kay felt as if he were sinking into a drift of snow.

"Are you still cold?" she asked, and then she kissed his brow. Oh! Her kiss was colder than ice. It went to his heart, although that was half frozen already, and he thought he would die. This feeling, however, only lasted for a moment. Straight afterward he was quite well and no longer felt the intense cold around.

"My sled! Do not forget my sled!" He thought about that straight away. So they fastened it to one of the white birds that flew behind with it on his back. The Snow Queen kissed Kay again, and he entirely forgot little Gerda, her grandmother, and everyone at home.

"Now you must have no more kisses," she said, "or I shall kiss you to death."

Kay looked at her. She was very beautiful; a more intelligent, more lovely countenance he could not imagine. She no longer appeared to him as cold as ice, as she had when she sat outside the window and beckoned to him. In his eyes she was perfect and now he felt no fear. He told her how

good he was at arithmetic, even fractions, and how he knew the number of square miles of every country and the number of people who lived in different towns. She smiled, and then it occurred to him that perhaps he did not yet know so very much after all. He looked up into the wide, wide space, and she flew with him high into the black cloud where the storm was raging.

They flew over woods and over lakes, over sea and over land. Beneath them the cold wind whistled, wolves howled, the snow glittered, and a black crow flew cawing over the plain. But above them the moon shone cold and clear.

Thus did Kay spend the long, long winter night, and all day he slept at the feet of the Snow Queen.

# THE ENCHANTED
# FLOWER GARDEN

But how did little Gerda get on when Kay never returned? Where could he be? No one knew. The boys said they had seen him fasten his sled to a large sleigh that had driven into the street and then swept through the gates of the town. But no one knew where they had gone, and many tears were shed over him. Gerda wept and wept, for the boys said he must have been drowned in the river. Oh, how long and dismal the winter days were!

At last the spring came, with its warm sunshine.

"Alas, Kay is dead and gone," said Gerda.

"I do not believe it," said the sunshine.

"He is dead and gone," she said to the swallows.

"We do not believe it," they replied, and after a time Gerda herself did not believe it.

"I will put on my new red shoes," she said one morning, "the ones that Kay has never seen, and then I will go down to the river and ask after him."

It was quite early. She kissed her old grandmother, who was still sleeping, put on her red shoes, and went alone through the gates of the town toward the river.

"Is it true," she said, "that you have taken my friend away? I will give you my red shoes if you will give him back to me!"

And the waves of the river flowed toward her in a strange way, so she thought that they were going to accept her offer. She took off her red shoes—though she prized them more than anything else she possessed—and threw them into the stream. But the waves bore them back to her, as though they would not take them from her because they had not got Kay.

Gerda thought she had not thrown the shoes far enough, so she stepped into a little boat that lay among the reeds by the shore and, standing at the farthest end of it, threw them far into the water. The boat was not fastened, and the movement inside it made it glide away from the shore. Seeing this she hurried back to the other end, but by the time she reached it, it was more than a yard from the land. She could not escape, and the boat moved on.

Gerda was very frightened and began to

cry, but no one besides the sparrows heard her. They could not carry her back to the land, but they flew along the banks and sang, as if to comfort her, "Here we are, here we are!" as the boat followed the stream.

"Perhaps the river will take me to Kay," she thought. At last she glided past a large cherry orchard, in which there was a cottage with a thatched roof and curious red-and-blue windows. Two wooden soldiers stood at the door, and they stood to attention when they saw the little vessel approach.

Gerda called to them, thinking they were alive, but they made no answer. She came close up to them, for the stream carried the boat toward the land.

She called still louder, and an old lady came out of the house, supporting herself on a crutch. She wore a large hat with the most beautiful flowers painted on it.

"Poor little child!" said the old woman. "The mighty river has indeed brought you a long way." And she walked right into the water, seized the boat with her crutch, drew it to land, and took Gerda out. Gerda was glad to be on dry land again, although she was a little afraid of the strange old lady.

"Come and tell me who you are and how you came here," said the old lady.

So Gerda told her everything and the old lady shook her head and said, "Hum! hum!" And when Gerda asked if she had seen Kay, the lady said that he had not arrived yet but that he would be sure to come soon and in the meantime Gerda must not be too sad. She could stay with her and eat her cherries and look at her flowers, which were prettier than any picture book, and each flower would tell her a story.

Then the old lady took Gerda by the hand and they went together into the cottage, and the old lady shut the door. A plate of very fine cherries was placed on a table in the middle and Gerda was allowed to eat as many as she liked. While she was eating them, the old lady combed Gerda's hair with a golden comb.

"I have long wished for a dear little girl like you," said the old lady. "We will see if we can live very happily together." And, as she combed Gerda's hair, Gerda thought less and less of Kay, for the old lady was an enchantress. She did not, however, practice magic for the sake of mischief but merely for her own amusement.

Now she wanted to keep Gerda to live with her very much and feared that if Gerda saw her roses she would be reminded of her own flowers and of Kay. So the old lady went out into the garden and waved her crutch over all her rosebushes, which, although they were covered with leaves and blossoms, immediately sank into the black earth.

Then she led Gerda into the garden. Flowers of all seasons and all climates grew there in profusion. Gerda danced with delight and played among the flowers till the sun set behind the cherry trees. Then a small

bed, with crimson silk cushions and a mattress stuffed with blue violet-leaves, was made ready, and she slept soundly there and had sweet dreams.

The next day she played again among the flowers in the warm sunshine, and she spent many more days in the same way. She knew every flower in the garden, but, numerous as they were, it seemed to her that one was missing, though she could not remember which. Then one day she was sitting looking at the old lady's hat, which was the one with the flowers painted on it, and, behold, the loveliest flower among them was a rose. The old lady had entirely forgotten that it was there.

"Why," cried Gerda, "there are no roses in the garden!" She ran from one bed to another looking everywhere, but she couldn't find a rose anywhere. She sat down and wept, and it so happened that her tears

fell on a spot where a rose tree had stood before. As soon as her warm tears had wet the earth, the bush sprang up again, as fresh as it was before it had sunk into the ground. Gerda threw her arms round it, kissed the flowers, and immediately remembered Kay. "Oh, how could I stay here so long!" she exclaimed. "I left home to look for Kay. Do you know where he is?" she asked the roses. "Is he dead?"

"He is not dead," said the roses. "We have been down in the earth. The dead are there, but not Kay."

"Thank you," said Gerda, and she went to the other flowers and asked, "Do you know where Kay is?"

But every flower stood in the sunshine dreaming its own dream. They told their stories to Gerda, but none of them knew anything about Kay.

So away she ran to the end of the garden.

The gate was closed, but she pressed down upon the rusty lock until it broke. The gate sprang open, and Gerda ran barefoot out into the world. She looked back three times; there was no one following her. She ran till she could run no longer and then sat down to rest upon a large stone. Looking round everywhere she saw that summer was over and it was now late in the autumn. She had not noticed this in the enchanted garden where it was sunny and there were flowers all the year round.

"How long I must have stayed there!" said Gerda. "So it's autumn now. Well, then, there is no time to lose," and she rose to go on her way.

Oh, how sore and weary her feet were! And everything round about looked so cold and barren. The long willow leaves had already turned yellow and the dew trickled down from them like water. The sloe alone bore fruit, and its berries were sharp and bitter. That day, the world seemed cold and gray and sad.

# THE PRINCE
# AND THE PRINCESS

Gerda soon had to stop and rest again. Suddenly a large raven hopped upon the snow in front of her, saying, "Caw!—Caw!—Good day!—Good day!" He sat for some time, eyeing the little girl and wagging his head. Then he came forward to talk to her and ask her where she was going all alone. Gerda told the raven the story of her life and fortunes, and asked if he had seen Kay.

And the raven nodded his head, half doubtfully, and said, "That is possible—possible."

"Do you think so?" exclaimed Gerda, and she hugged the raven so enthusiastically that she nearly squeezed him to death.

"Gently, gently!" said the raven. "I think I know. I think it may be Kay, but he has certainly forsaken you for the princess."

"Does he live with a princess?" asked Gerda.

"Listen to me," said the raven. "But it is so difficult to speak your language. Do you understand Ravenish? If so, I can tell you much better."

"No, I have never learned Ravenish," said Gerda. "But my grandmother knew it. Oh, how I wish I had learnt it from her!"

"Never mind," said the raven. "I will tell you as best I can.

"In the kingdom where we are now there dwells a very clever princess. Immediately after she came to the throne, she began to sing a new song, the point of which was '*Why should I not marry?*' 'There is some sense in this song!' she said, and she determined she would marry but declared that the man whom she would choose must be able to answer sensibly

whenever people spoke to him and must be good for something else besides merely looking grand. Believe me," continued the raven, "every word I say is true, for my sweetheart hops about the palace as she pleases and she has told me all this.

"Proclamations, adorned with borders of hearts, were immediately sent out, proclaiming that every well-favored youth was free to go to the palace, and that whoever should talk and show himself intelligent and at ease with the princess would be the one she would choose for her husband.

"The people all crowded to the palace, but it was no use. The young men could speak well enough while they were outside the palace gates, but when they went in and saw the royal guard in silver uniform and the servants on the staircase in gold and the spacious rooms all lighted up, they were quite speechless. They stood before the throne where the princess sat, and when she spoke to them they could only repeat the last word she had uttered. It was just as though they had been struck dumb the moment they entered the palace, for as soon as they got out they could talk fast enough. There was a regular procession."

"But Kay, when did he come?" asked Gerda. "Was he among the crowd?"

"Presently, presently; we have just come to him. On the third day a youth with neither horse nor carriage arrived. Gaily he marched up to the palace. His eyes sparkled like yours. He had long, beautiful hair but was very meanly clad."

"That was Kay!" exclaimed Gerda. "Oh, then I have found him!" And she clapped her hands with delight.

"He carried a knapsack on his back," said the raven.

"No, not a knapsack," said Gerda, "a sled, for he had a sled with him."

"It is possible," rejoined the raven. "I did not look very closely, but I heard from my beloved that when he entered the palace gates and saw the royal guard in silver and the servants in gold upon the staircase, he did not seem in the least confused. He nodded pleasantly and said to them, 'It must be very tedious standing out here. I'm glad I'm going in.' The halls glistened with light; it was just the sort of place that makes a man solemn and silent, and the youth's boots creaked horribly—yet he was not at all afraid."

"That certainly was Kay!" said Gerda. "I know he had new boots: I have heard them creak in my grandmother's room."

"They really did make a noise," said the raven, "but he went merrily up to the princess, who was sitting on a pearl as large as a spinning wheel.

"The young man spoke as well as I speak when I speak in Ravenish. He did not come to woo her, he said, he had only come to hear the wisdom of the princess. And he liked her very much, and she liked him in return."

"Yes, to be sure, that was Kay," said Gerda. "He was so clever, he could do arithmetic in his head, even fractions! Oh, will you take me to the palace?"

"Ah! That is easily said," replied the raven, "but how is it to be done? I will talk it over with my sweetheart. She will advise us what to do.

"Wait for me at the trellis over there," said the raven. He wagged his head and away he flew.

He did not return until late that evening. "Caw, caw," he said. "My sweetheart greets you kindly and sends you a piece of bread that she took from the kitchen. There is plenty there, and you must certainly be hungry. As you have bare feet, the royal guard would never permit you to enter the palace. But do not weep, you shall go there. My sweetheart knows a little back staircase leading to the bedrooms, and she also knows where to find the key."

So they went into the garden and down the grand avenue, and, when the lights in the palace had been put out one by one, the raven took Gerda to a back door that stood half open. Oh, how Gerda's heart beat with fear and expectation! It was just as though she were about to do something wrong, although she only wanted to know whether Kay was really there. She would see if his smile was the same. He would be so glad to see her, to hear how far she had come for his sake, and how everyone at home missed him.

They climbed the staircase. A small lamp placed on a cabinet gave a glimmer of light, and on the floor stood the tame raven, who first turned her head on all sides and then looked at Gerda, who curtsied as her grand-mother had taught her.

"My betrothed has told me much about you, my good young maiden," said the tame raven. "Your adventures are extremely in-teresting. If you will take the lamp, I will show you the way."

They entered the first room. Its walls were covered with rose-colored satin and embroi-dered with gold flowers. Some dreams rus-tled past them, but so quickly that Gerda could not see them. Each room that they went through was more splendid than the room before, until at last they reached the sleeping hall. In the center of this room stood a pillar of gold like the stem of a large palm tree whose leaves of costly glass made up the ceiling. Hanging down from the tree

on thick golden stalks were two beds in the form of lilies. One was white, and in it rested the princess. The other was red, and in it Gerda hoped to find her playfellow Kay. She bent aside one of the red leaves and saw a neck. Oh, it must be Kay! She called him by his name aloud and held the lamp close to him. The dreams rushed by. He awoke, turned his head, but behold!—it was not Kay.

The princess looked out from under the white lily petals and asked what was the matter. Then Gerda wept and told her the whole story and what the ravens had done for her.

"You poor child!" said the prince and princess, and then they praised the ravens and said they were not angry with them, but that they weren't to do it again. This once, however, they should be rewarded.

"Would you like to fly away freely to the woods?" asked the princess, addressing the ravens, "or would you rather have appointments as Court-Ravens with the benefits belonging to the kitchen, such as crumbs?"

And both the ravens bowed low and chose the appointment at court, for they thought of their old age and said it would be so comfortable to be provided for. Then the prince rose and made Gerda sleep in his bed.

The next day she was dressed from head to foot in beautiful clothes. She was invited to stay at the palace, but she begged only for a carriage and a horse and a pair of boots. All she wanted was to go back into the wide world to look for Kay.

They gave her the boots and a muff as well, and as soon as she was ready, a carriage of pure gold drove up to the palace door. The coachman, footman, and outriders all wore gold crowns. The princess and prince themselves helped her into the carriage and wished her success, and the wood raven, who was now married, accompanied her the first three miles.

"Farewell, farewell!" cried the prince and princess. Gerda wept, and the raven wept out of sympathy. Then he flew up to the branch of a tree and flapped his black wings at the coach till it was out of sight.

# THE ROBBER-MAIDEN

They drove through the dark, dark forest. The carriage shone like a torch, and unfortunately its brightness attracted the eyes of the robbers who lived in the shadows of the forest.

"That is gold!" they cried. They rushed forward, seized the horses, stabbed the outriders, coachman, and footman, and dragged Gerda out of the carriage.

"She is plump, she is pretty," said the old robber-wife, who had a long, bristly beard and eyebrows hanging like bushes over her eyes. "She is like a fat little lamb, and how smartly she is dressed!" And she drew out her dagger, which glittered most terribly.

"Oh, oh!" cried the woman for, the very moment she had lifted her dagger to stab Gerda, her own wild and willful daughter had jumped on her back and bitten her ear violently. "You naughty child!" said the mother.

"She shall play with me," said the young robber-maiden. "She shall give me her muff and pretty frock, and sleep with me in my bed." Then she bit her mother again, till the robber-wife sprang up and shrieked with pain, while the robbers all laughed, saying, "Look at her playing with her daughter."

So spoiled was the robber-maiden that she always got her own way, and she and Gerda sat together in the carriage and drove farther into the wood. The robber-maiden was about as tall as Gerda but much stronger. She had broad shoulders and very dark skin; her eyes were quite black and had an almost melancholy expression. She put her arm around Gerda's waist and said, "She shan't kill you so long as I love you. Aren't you a princess?"

"No," said Gerda. And then she told her all that had happened to her and how much she loved Kay.

The robber-maiden looked earnestly in her face, shook her head, and said, "She shall not kill you even if I do quarrel with you. Indeed, I would rather do it myself!" And she dried Gerda's tears and put both her hands into the pretty muff that was so soft and warm.

The carriage stopped at last in the middle of the courtyard of the robbers' castle. This castle was half ruined. Crows and ravens flew out of the openings, and some fearfully large

bulldogs, looking as if they could devour a man in a moment, jumped round the carriage. They were forbidden to bark.

Gerda and the robber-maiden entered a large, smokey hall, where a tremendous fire was blazing on the stone floor. A huge cauldron full of soup was boiling on the fire, while hares and rabbits were roasting on the spit.

"You shall sleep with me and my little pets tonight," said the robber-maiden. Then they had some food and afterward went to the corner, where there was some straw and a piece of carpet. Nearly a hundred pigeons were perched around them. They were asleep but woke when the two young maidens approached.

"These all belong to me," said Gerda's companion, and seizing hold of one of the nearest, she held the poor bird by the feet and swung it round. "Kiss it," she said, flapping it into Gerda's face. "The rabble from the wood sit up there," she continued, pointing to a number of sticks fastened across a hole in the wall. "Those are wood-pigeons. They would fly away if I didn't keep them shut up. And here is my old favorite!" She pulled forward a reindeer who wore a bright copper ring round his neck, by which he was fastened to a large stone. "We have to chain him up or he would run away from us. Every evening I tickle his neck with my sharp dagger. It makes him so frightened of me!" And the robber-maiden drew out a long dagger from a gap in the wall

and ran it down the reindeer's throat. The poor animal struggled and kicked, but the girl laughed, and then she pulled Gerda into bed with her.

"Are you going to keep the dagger in your hand while you sleep?" asked Gerda, looking timidly at the dangerous weapon.

"I always sleep with my dagger by my side," replied the robber-maiden. "One never knows what may happen. But now tell me all over again what you told me before about Kay and the reason for your coming into the wide world all by yourself."

So Gerda told her story again and the imprisoned wood-pigeons listened, but the others were fast asleep. The robber-maiden threw one arm round Gerda's neck and, holding the dagger with the other, was also soon asleep. But Gerda could not close her eyes throughout the night. She didn't know what would become of her or whether she would even be allowed to live. The robbers sat round the fire drinking and singing. Oh, it was a dreadful night for poor Gerda!

Then the wood-pigeons spoke, "Coo, coo, coo—we have seen Kay. A white bird carried his sled. He was in the Snow Queen's sleigh, which passed through the wood whilst we sat in our nest. She breathed on us young ones, and all died of her icy breath except for us two—coo, coo, coo!"

"What are you saying?" cried Gerda. "Where was the Snow Queen going? Do you know anything about where she lives?"

"She traveled most probably to Lapland, where there are ice and snow all year round. Ask the reindeer."

"Yes, ice and snow are there all through the year. It is a glorious land," said the reindeer. "There, free and happy, one can roam through the wide sparkling valleys. There the Snow Queen has her summer tent. Her strong castle is a long way off, near the North Pole on an island called Spitzbergen."

"Oh, Kay, dear Kay!" sighed Gerda.

When morning came Gerda told the robber-maiden what the wood pigeons had said, and the robber-maiden looked serious for a moment. Then she nodded her head. "Do you know where Lapland is?" she asked the reindeer.

"Who should know better than I!" returned the animal, his eyes sparkling. "Lapland is where I was born. How often have I run over the wild icy plains there!"

"Listen to me!" said the robber-maiden to Gerda. "You see all the men are going out now, but my mother will stay behind. Toward noon she will drink a little out of the great jug, and after that she will sleep. Then I will do something for you."

When her mother was fast asleep, the robber-maiden went up to the reindeer and said, "I should have great pleasure in stroking you a few more times with my sharp dagger, for you look so comic. But never mind; I will undo your chain and help you to escape on condition that you run as fast as you can to Lapland and take this young girl to the castle of the Snow Queen, where her playfellow is. You must have heard her story, for she speaks loudly enough and you're good at eavesdropping!"

The reindeer bounded with joy, and the robber-maiden lifted Gerda on his back, taking care to bind her on firmly as well as to give her a little cushion to sit on. "And here," she said, "are your fur boots. You will need them in that cold country. The muff I will keep for myself; it is too pretty to part with. But you won't be frozen. Here are my mother's huge gloves. They reach up to the elbow. Put them on— now your hands look as clumsy as my old mother's!"

Gerda shed tears of joy.

"I cannot bear to see you crying," said the robber-maiden. "You ought to look glad. See, here are two loaves and a piece of bacon for you, so you're not hungry on the way."

She fastened this food on the reindeer's back as well, opened the door, called away the great dogs, and then, cutting the reindeer's rope with her dagger, shouted to him, "Now then, run! But take good care of Gerda."

Gerda stretched out her hands to the robber-maiden and said good-bye, and the reindeer bounded through the forest, over mud and stone, over desert and heath, over meadow and moor.

The wolves howled and the ravens shrieked. There was a noise in the sky—*tcho, tcho,*—and a red light flashed. It was almost as though the sky were sneezing.

"Those are my dear old northern lights," said the reindeer. "Look at them, aren't they beautiful?" And he ran faster than ever, night and day. They ate the loaves and the bacon, and then, at last, they were in Lapland.

# THE LAPLAND WOMAN
# AND THE FINLAND WOMAN

They stopped at a little hut. It was a miserable building. The roof very nearly touched the ground and the door was so low that anyone who wanted to go in or out had to crawl on hands and knees. No one was at home except an old Lapland woman who was busy boiling fish over an oil lamp. The reindeer told her Gerda's whole story—but not, however, until he had told her his own, which seemed to him to be much more important. Poor Gerda, meanwhile, was so overpowered by the cold that she could not speak.

"Ah, poor thing!" said the Lapland woman. "You still have a long way to go. You have a hundred miles to run before you get to Finland. The Snow Queen lives there and burns blue lights every evening. I will write a few words on a piece of dried fish, for I haven't any paper, and you may take it with you to the wise Finland woman who lives there. She will advise you better than I can."

So when Gerda had warmed herself through and eaten some food, the Lapland woman wrote a few words on the dried fish, told Gerda to take great care of it, and firmly bound her once more on the reindeer's back.

They sped onward. The wonderful northern lights, which were now the loveliest, brightest blue, shone all through the night, and with the help of these they arrived in Finland. They knocked on the wise

Finland woman's chimney, for she had no door to her house.

It was very hot inside—so much so that the wise woman wore scarcely any clothes. She was small and very dirty. She loosened Gerda's dress, took off her fur boots and thick gloves, laid a piece of ice on the reindeer's head, and then read what was written on the dried fish. She read it three times. After reading it three times she knew it by heart, so she threw the fish into the porridge pot, for it would make a very excellent supper and she never wasted anything.

The reindeer then repeated his own story, and when that was finished he told her about Gerda's adventures, and the wise woman's eyes twinkled, but she did not speak.

"Won't you mix Gerda that wonderful draught that will give her the strength of twelve men, so she can overcome the Snow Queen?" asked the reindeer.

"The strength of twelve men!" repeated the wise woman. "That would be a lot of good!" And she walked away, drew out a large parchment roll from a shelf, and began to read. She read so intently that perspiration ran down her forehead.

At last her eyes began to twinkle again, and she drew the reindeer into a corner and, putting a fresh piece of ice upon his head, whispered, "Kay is still with the Snow Queen, where he finds everything so much to his liking that he believes it to be the best place in the world. But that is because he has

a glass splinter in his heart and a glass splinter in his eye. Until he has got rid of them he will never feel human and the Snow Queen will always have power over him."

"But can't you give something to Gerda that will overcome all these evil influences?"

"I can give her no power as great as that which she already possesses. Her power is greater than ours because it comes from her heart, from her being an innocent and loving child. If it cannot give her access to the Snow Queen's palace and help her to free Kay's eye and heart from the glass fragment, then we can do nothing. The Snow Queen's

garden is two miles away. Carry Gerda there and put her down by the bush bearing red berries that is half covered with snow. Don't waste any time, and hurry back!"

Then the wise woman lifted Gerda onto the reindeer's back, and away they went.

"Oh, I've left my boots behind! I left my gloves behind!" cried Gerda, but it was too late. The cold was piercing, but the reindeer dared not stop. He ran on until he reached the bush with the red berries. Here he set Gerda down, kissed her with tears rolling down his cheeks, and ran quickly back again, which was the best thing he could do. And there stood poor Gerda, without shoes, without gloves, alone in that barren country, that terribly icy-cold Finland.

She ran on as fast as she could. A whole regiment of snowflakes came to meet her. They did not fall from the sky, which was cloudless and bright with the northern lights. They ran straight along the ground, and the farther Gerda advanced, the larger they grew. Then she remembered how large and strange the snowflakes had appeared to her the day she had looked at them through the magnifying glass. These, however, were very much larger. They were, in fact, the Snow Queen's guards, and their shapes were the strangest imaginable. Some looked like great ugly porcupines, others like snakes rolled into knots with their heads peering out, and others like little fat bears with bristling hair. Gerda began to say a prayer, and it was so cold

that she could see her own breath, which, as
it escaped from her mouth, rose into the air
like steam.

As the cold grew more intense, the steam
grew more dense, and at length it took the
form of bright little angels, which, as they
touched the earth, became larger. They
wore helmets on their heads and carried
shields and spears. Their numbers increased
so rapidly that, by the time Gerda had
finished her prayer, a whole group of them
stood round her. They thrust their spears
among the horrible snowflakes that fell into
thousands of pieces, and Gerda walked on
protected and unhurt. The angels touched
her hands and feet, and then she scarcely felt
the cold and approached the Snow Queen's
palace fearlessly.

But meanwhile, what of Kay? What was
he doing? He was certainly not thinking of
Gerda. Least of all did he think that she was
now standing at the palace gate.

# THE SNOW QUEEN'S PALACE

The walls of the palace were made of driven snow, its doors and windows of cutting winds. There were a hundred halls, the largest of which was many miles long, all illuminated by the northern lights. They were all alike: vast, empty, icily cold, and dazzlingly white. In the middle of the empty, interminable snow lay a frozen lake. It was broken into exactly a thousand pieces, and these pieces were so exactly alike that it might well be thought a work of more than human skill. The Snow Queen always sat in the center of this lake when she was at home.

Kay played among the icy fragments, joining them together in every possible way just as people do with Chinese puzzles. He had become quite blue with cold; in fact, he was almost black, but he did not notice it for the Snow Queen had kissed away the shrinking feeling he used to experience, and his heart was like a lump of ice. Kay could make the most curious and complete figures—and in his eyes these figures were of the utmost importance. He often spelled out whole words, but there was one word he could never succeed in forming. It was *Eternity*. The Snow Queen had said to him, "When you can put that word together, you shall become your own master, and I will give you the whole world and a new pair of skates as well."

But he could never do it.

"Now I am going to the warm countries," said the Snow Queen one day. "I shall sail through the air and look into the black cauldrons." She meant the volcanoes Etna and Vesuvius. "I shall whiten them a little." So she flew away, leaving Kay sitting all alone in the large empty hall of ice. He looked at the fragments and thought and thought, till his head ached. He sat so still and stiff that he looked as though he was frozen solid.

Just then Gerda passed through the palace gates. The winds blew keenly, but she repeated her prayer and they ceased as she entered the huge empty hall. There she saw Kay. She flew to him, fell upon his neck, held him fast, and cried, "Kay! Dear, dear Kay! I have found you at last!"

But he sat as still as before—cold, silent, motionless. Gerda began to cry, shedding warm tears that fell on Kay and found their way to his heart. They thawed the ice and dissolved the tiny fragment of glass within it. He looked at her, and she sang her hymn:

*Our roses bloom and fade away,*
*Our Infant Lord abides always;*
*May we be blessed His face to see,*
*And ever little children be!*

Then Kay burst into tears. He wept till the glass splinter floated in his eye and fell with his tears. He knew his old companion immediately and exclaimed with joy, "Gerda, my dear Gerda, where have you been all this time? And where have I been?"

He looked around him. "How cold it is here! How wide and empty!" Then he hugged Gerda, while she laughed and wept. Even the pieces of ice took part in their joy. They danced about merrily, and when they were weary they lay down forming of their own accord the word *Eternity*, which made Kay his own master.

Gerda kissed his cheeks, and immediately they became as fresh and glowing as ever. She kissed his eyes, and they sparkled like her own. She kissed his hands and feet, and

he was once more healthy and merry. The Snow Queen might come home as soon as she liked—it didn't matter. Kay's right to his freedom stood written on the lake in bright icy characters.

They took each other by the hand and wandered out of the palace. As they walked on, the winds were hushed into a calm and the sun burst out in splendor from among the dark storm clouds. When they arrived at the bush with the red berries, they found the reindeer waiting for them. He had brought another younger reindeer with him, whose udders were full and who gladly gave warm milk to refresh them.

Then the two reindeer carried Kay and Gerda back to the little hothouse of the wise woman of Finland, where they warmed themselves and were told the best way to make the long journey home. Afterward they went to the Lapland woman, who made them some new clothes and provided them with a small sleigh.

The whole party now traveled on together until they came to the edge of Lapland. Just where the green leaves began to sprout, the Lapland woman and the two reindeer took their leave. "Farewell, farewell!" they all said. The first birds Kay and Gerda had seen for a long, long time began to sing their pretty songs, and the trees of the forest were heavy with bright green leaves. Suddenly the green boughs parted and a spirited horse galloped up. Gerda knew it well, for it was one that had been harnessed to her golden coach. On it sat a young girl wearing a bright scarlet cap with pistols on the holster before her. It was none other than the robber-maiden! Fed up with her home in the forest, she had taken to traveling, first to the north and afterward to other parts of the world. She at once recognized Gerda, and Gerda had certainly not forgotten her. They hugged each other joyfully.

"A fine gentleman you are, to be sure, you graceless young truant!" she said to Kay. "I should like to know whether you deserved anyone running to the end of the world on your behalf."

But Gerda stroked her cheeks and asked after the prince and princess.

"They have gone traveling into foreign countries," replied the robber-maiden.

"And the raven?" asked Gerda.

"Ah! The raven is dead. Now his sweetheart is a widow, she hops about with a piece of flannel wound round her leg. She moans most sadly and chatters more than ever! But tell me now all that has happened to you and how you managed to pick up your old playfellow."

And Gerda and Kay told their story.

*"Snip-snap-snurre-basselurre!"* said the robber-maiden. She pressed the hands of both, promised that if ever she passed through their town she would pay them a visit, and then said good-bye and rode off.

Kay and Gerda walked on hand in hand, and wherever they went it was spring, beautiful spring, with its bright flowers and green leaves. They arrived at a large town, the church bells were ringing merrily, and they immediately recognized the high towers rising into the sky. It was the town where their families lived. Happily they passed through the streets and stopped at the door of Gerda's grandmother.

They walked up the stairs together and entered the well-known room. The clock said, "Tick, tock!" and the hands moved as before. They could only find one difference, and that was in themselves, for they saw that they were now grown-up people. The rose trees on the roof blossomed in front of the open window, and there beneath them stood the children's stools. Kay and Gerda went and sat down, still holding each other by the hand. They forgot the cold, hollow splendor of the Snow Queen's palace; it seemed like an unpleasant dream. Gerda's grandmother, now old, sat in the bright sunshine and read these words from the Bible, "Unless ye become as little children, ye shall not enter into the kingdom of heaven."

And Kay and Gerda gazed on each other, and all at once they understood the words of their hymn:

> *Our roses bloom and fade away,*
> *Our Infant Lord abides always;*
> *May we be blessed His face to see,*
> *And ever little children be!*

There they both sat, grown up and yet children—children at heart—and it was summer, beautiful, warm summer.